FROG ON HIS OWN

by Mercer Mayer

PUFFIN BOOKS

For Father Yonov
and his family

Library of Congress Catalog Card Number: 73-6017
First Pied Piper Printing 1980
Manufactured in China by South China Printing Co.
COBE
18 20 19
A Pied Piper Book is a registered trademark of Dial Books for Young Readers,
a division of Penguin Books USA Inc.
® TM 1,163,686 and ® TM 1,054,312
FROG ON HIS OWN is published in a hardcover edition by
Dial Books for Young Readers, 345 Hudson Street, New York, New York 10014
ISBN 0-14-054634-0

CITY
PARK

NO
SWIMMING

CHIC

CHIC

PUT TRASH
HERE

EXIT